For Kian, Louis, Wayne and Terry

SIMON & SCHUSTER BOOKS FOR YOUNG READERS
An imprint of Simon & Schuster Children's Publishing Division
1230 Avenue of the Americas, New York, New York 10020
Copyright © 2011 by Emily Gravett
Originally published in Great Britain in 2011 by Macmillan Children's Books,
Published by arrangement with Macmillan Publisher's Limited.
First U.S. edition 2013
For information about special discounts for bulk purchases, please contact
Simon & Schuster Special Sales at 1-866-506-1949 or business@simonandschuster.com.
The Simon & Schuster Speakers Bureau can bring authors to your live event.
For more information or to book an event, contact the Simon & Schuster Speakers Bureau
at 1-866-248-3049 or visit our website at www.simonspeakers.com.
The text for this book is set in Aperto.
The illustrations for this book are rendered in oil-based pencil and watercolor.
Manufactured in China · 1212 WKT
2 4 6 8 10 9 7 5 3 1
Library of Congress Cataloging-in-Publication Data
Gravett, Emily.
Again! / Emily Gravett.—1st U.S. ed.
p. cm.
Summary: At bedtime, Cedric the dragon wants his mother
to read his favorite book again, and again, and again.
ISBN 978-1-4424-5231-2 (hardcover : alk. paper)
[1. Books and reading—Fiction. 2. Dragons—Fiction. 3. Bedtime—Fiction.] I. Title.
PZ7.G77577Ag 2013
[E]—dc23
2012003322

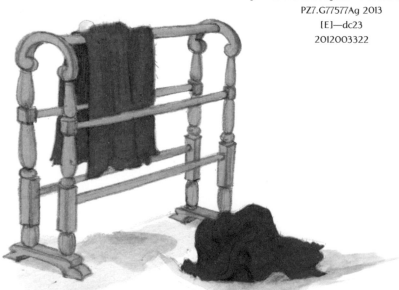

AGAIN!

Emily Gravett

SIMON & SCHUSTER BOOKS FOR YOUNG READERS
NEW YORK   LONDON   TORONTO   SYDNEY   NEW DELHI

For Kian, Louis, Wayne and Terry

SIMON & SCHUSTER BOOKS FOR YOUNG READERS
An imprint of Simon & Schuster Children's Publishing Division
1230 Avenue of the Americas, New York, New York 10020
Copyright © 2011 by Emily Gravett
Originally published in Great Britain in 2011 by Macmillan Children's Books,
Published by arrangement with Macmillan Publisher's Limited.
First U.S. edition 2013
SIMON & SCHUSTER BOOKS FOR YOUNG READERS is a trademark of Simon & Schuster, Inc.
For information about special discounts for bulk purchases, please contact
Simon & Schuster Special Sales at 1-866-506-1949 or business@simonandschuster.com.
The Simon & Schuster Speakers Bureau can bring authors to your live event.
For more information or to book an event, contact the Simon & Schuster Speakers Bureau
at 1-866-248-3049 or visit our website at www.simonspeakers.com.
The text for this book is set in Aperto.
The illustrations for this book are rendered in oil-based pencil and watercolor.
Manufactured in China · 1212 WKT
2 4 6 8 10 9 7 5 3 1
Library of Congress Cataloging-in-Publication Data
Gravett, Emily.
Again! / Emily Gravett.—1st U.S. ed.
p. cm.
Summary: At bedtime, Cedric the dragon wants his mother
to read his favorite book again, and again, and again.
ISBN 978-1-4424-5231-2 (hardcover : alk. paper)
[1. Books and reading—Fiction. 2. Dragons—Fiction. 3. Bedtime—Fiction.] I. Title.
PZ7.G77577Ag 2013
[E]—dc23
2012003322

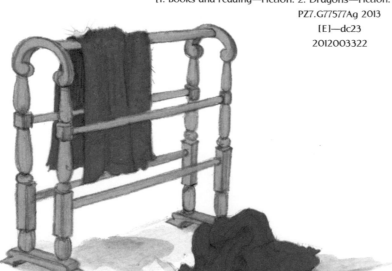

AGAIN!

Emily Gravett

SIMON & SCHUSTER BOOKS FOR YOUNG READERS

NEW YORK   LONDON   TORONTO   SYDNEY   NEW DELHI

It was nearly bedtime.

Cedric the dragon's a bright angry red.
He's never,
His whole life,
(Not once) been to bed.

At nighttime when everyone else is asleep,
He noisily prowls through the tower, then leaps
Down to the bridge to be nasty and sly,
And torment the trolls (who by nature are shy).

When that makes him hungry, he takes to the skies,
Grabbing princesses to turn into pies,
Or occasionally crumbles, or sometimes just toast
(If crumbles or pies would take too long to roast).

At the end of each day he shouts out this refrain:
"TOMORROW I'LL DO IT ALL OVER AGAIN!"

2

Again?

Cedric the dragon's a bright angry red.
He's never,
His whole life,
(Not once) been to bed.

At nighttime when Cedric SHOULD be asleep,
He noisily stomps through the tower, then leaps
Down to the bridge to say a big sorry,
For teasing the trolls (who do tend to worry).

When that makes him hungry, he takes out a pie,
Which he shares with the trolls. Then, heaving a sigh,
He goes home to his tower
And shouts out this refrain:
"TOMORROW I'LL DO IT ALL OVER AGAIN!"

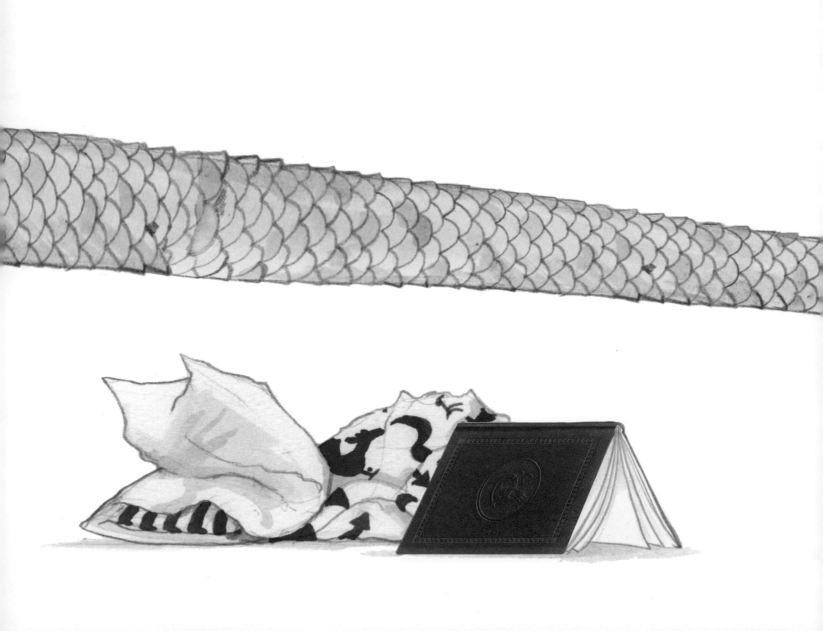

AGAIN!

Cedric the dragon's *a big sleepyhead.*
He's decided it's time
HE WAS REALLY IN BED.

He's made friends with the princess
And wished her good night,
The trolls are all happy,
The moon is out bright.

Now I'm closing the book and saying quite plain:

"TOMORROW I'll read it all over again."

AGAIN!

AGAIN!

edric the dragon *is* no longer red,

As Cedric . . .

the dragon's . . . asleep

. . . in . . . his . . . be . . . z z z   z

AGAIN!
AGAIN!
AGAIN!

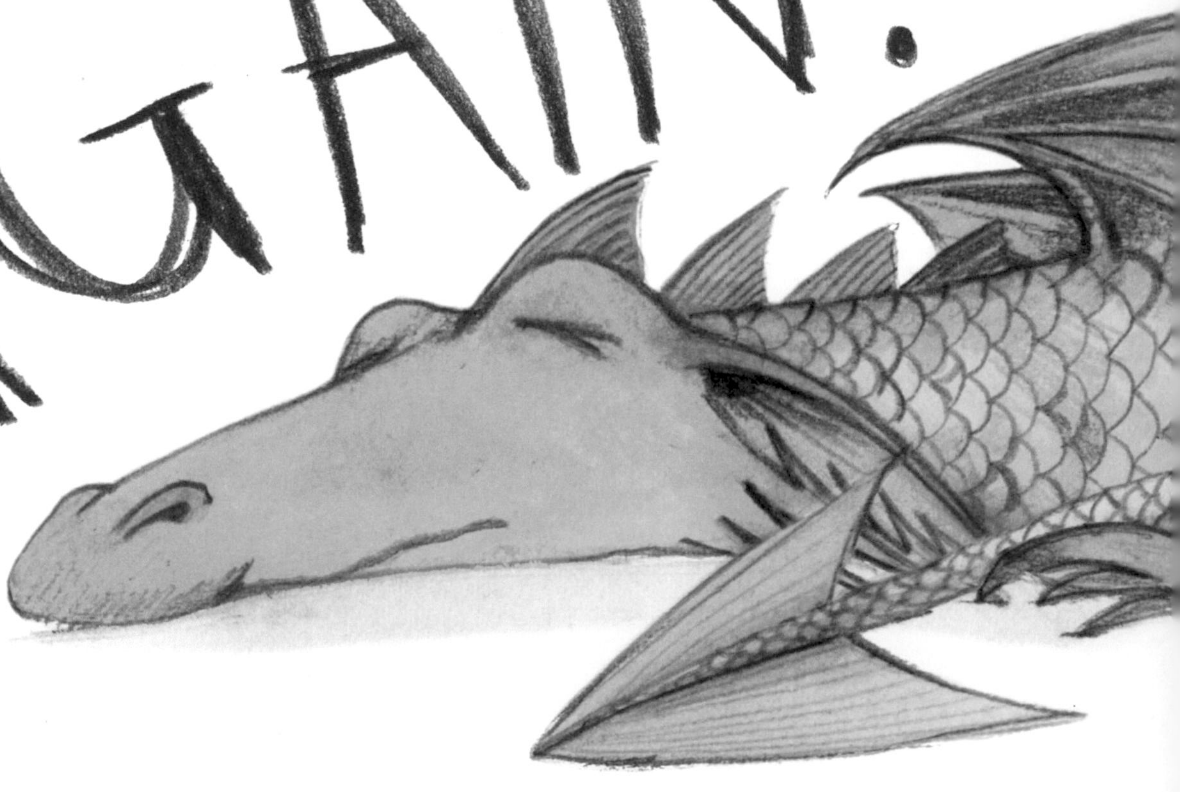

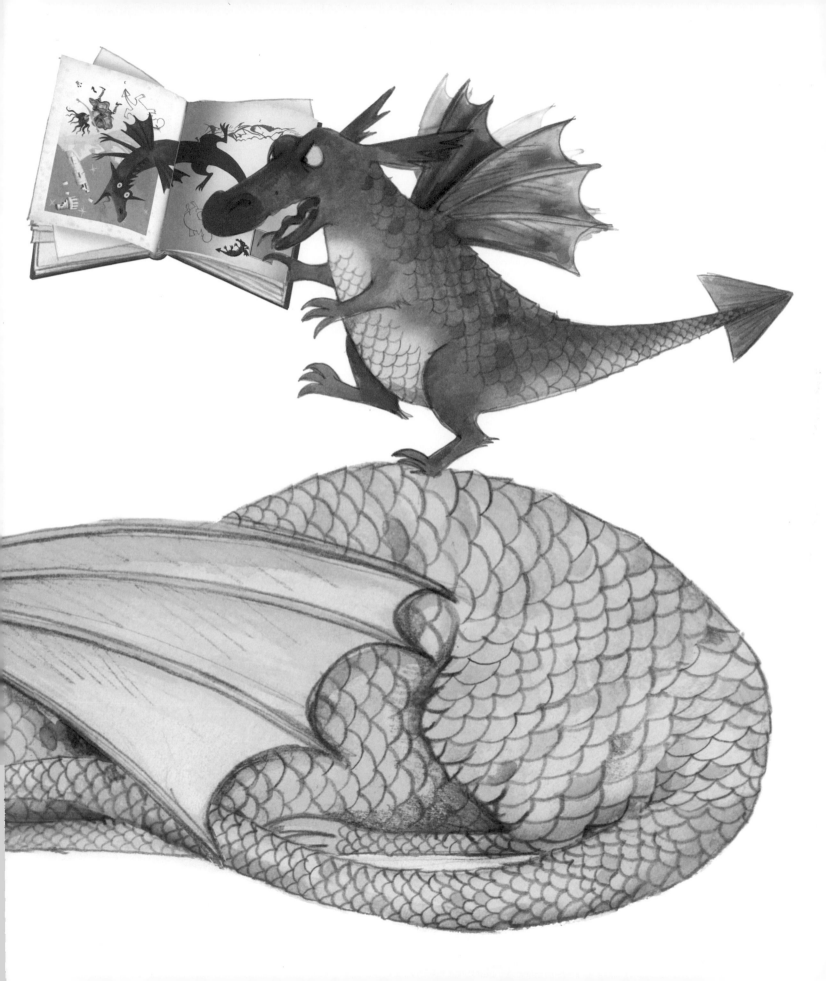

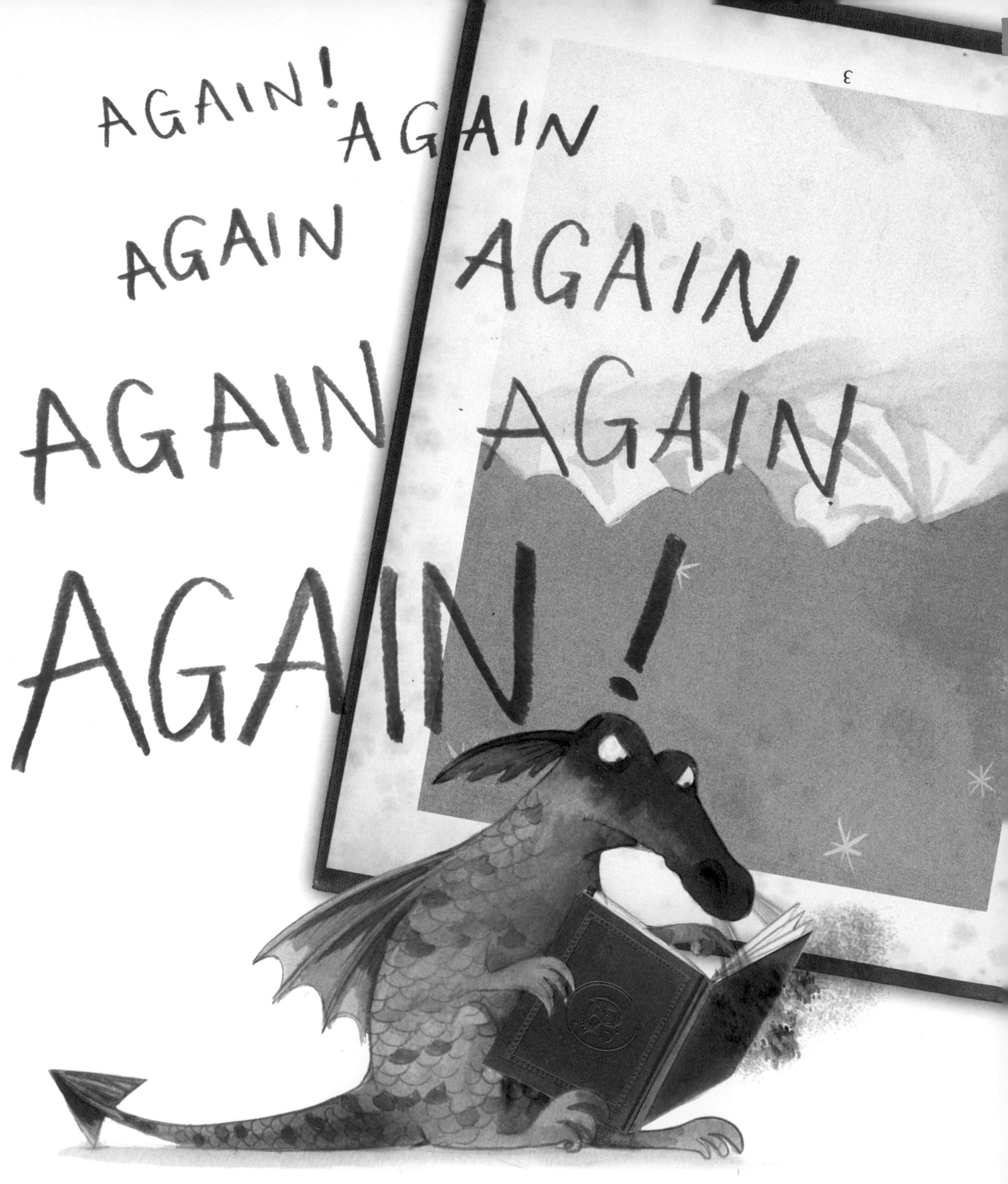
AGAIN! AGAIN
AGAIN AGAIN
AGAIN AGAIN
AGAIN!